# The Crystal Apple

written by
Barry Lock

with illustrations by
D M Cornish

## Stone Table Books

THE CRYSTAL APPLE

Copyright © 2020 Barry Lock. All rights reserved. Except for brief quotations in critical publications or reviews, no part of this book may be reproduced in any manner without prior written permission from the publisher. Write: Permissions, Wipf and Stock Publishers, 199 W. 8th Ave., Suite 3, Eugene, OR 97401.

Stone Table Books
An Imprint of Wipf and Stock Publishers
199 W. 8th Ave., Suite 3
Eugene, OR 97401

www.wipfandstock.com

PAPERBACK ISBN: 978-1-7252-6595-0
HARDCOVER ISBN: 978-1-7252-6593-6
EBOOK ISBN: 978-1-7252-6594-3

Manufactured in the U.S.A.    SEPTEMBER 22, 2020

Typesetting by Ben Morton
Cover and internal illustrations by D M Cornish

Dedicated with love to:
My sons Josh, Greg and Philip
who heard this story when they were boys.
And to my special grandchildren
Roya, Abigail, Corban, Isaac, Tobias,
Mahalia, Avalon, Josiah and Ezra.

**There was once** a rich and powerful king who lived with his son in a magnificent castle set high on a hill in the middle of his kingdom.

All around the castle was a beautiful apple orchard surrounded by high stone walls. The trees in this orchard were quite amazing and different to any other trees. Instead of ordinary green or red apples they produced apples of pure, dazzling crystal.

The remarkable thing about these beautiful, priceless apples was that they lasted forever. Anyone who had one would never part with it.

You might think that a king so powerful and rich would be greedy and selfish. But this king wasn't like that at all. He was a loving and generous king who wanted to share the good things he had with everyone in his kingdom.

One day the king sent messengers on fast horses to every part of his kingdom. In every town and village square they read out this message from the king: "To every person who kneels before me in the royal throne room and asks, I will give one of my precious crystal apples to be their very own forever." The message was signed by the king and sealed with the king's royal ring.

Time went by and many journeyed to the king's castle. There, in the magnificent royal throne room, kneeling before the king, they received a crystal apple to be their very own. However, there was a man who lived in the village across the valley who did not trust the king. His name was Mr. Allman. Even though he wanted a crystal apple more than anything else in the world, he didn't believe the king.

"How could anyone, even someone as rich and powerful as the king, give away a priceless, crystal apple as a gift?" he said to everyone in the village.

"No, I don't trust the king at all. This is a trick to trap me into serving him forever."

One day the king was standing on his balcony looking out across his kingdom and enjoying the shimmering light from the crystal apples in his orchard. Suddenly, he noticed movement below in the bushes by the castle wall.

As he watched, he saw someone squeeze through a hole in the wall behind the bushes. Then he saw a man creeping toward the crystal apple trees. The man looked over his left shoulder and then his right, then began climbing up into one of the trees. Just as he was reaching out to grab one of the crystal apples he saw two royal guards marching around the corner of the castle. He leapt from the tree, turned and ran back to the safety of the bushes and disappeared through the hole in the wall.

The king's heart was heavy because he recognised Mr. Allman from the village across the valley. The king was sad because, as everyone in the kingdom knew, there was a penalty for trying to steal a crystal apple. The thief would be banished to the lonely land of the Dark Powers which was ruled by the evil Darknor.

The next day, the king was standing on his balcony again. At his side was his son, the prince, whom he loved dearly. Once again the king saw movement in the bushes by the wall. Once again a figure squeezed his way through the hole and crept toward the trees. He looked over his left shoulder then his right and then began climbing. Just as he was reaching to grasp a crystal apple the king called out, "Allman!"

Mr. Allman stopped moving and peered around to look up through the dazzling light of the orchard toward the king's balcony, his face grim.

"Why try to steal what you could be given as a gift if you would only come to me?" called the king.

"I don't trust you," Allman shouted, shaking a clenched fist at the king. "It's just your way of tricking me into serving you forever. I won't fall for your trap."

With that he leapt from the tree, turned, and ran to the bushes and disappeared through the hole in the wall.

When the king saw Allman disappear through the bushes he hung his head with a deep sigh.

"He's so angry, Father," the prince said. "Will he ever come to us?

"I don't want anyone banished to the land of Dark Powers, not Allman, not anyone," replied the king.

"But he tried to steal one of your crystal apples. And he shook his fist and shouted at you."

The king was quiet for a moment, then he said in a clear, strong voice, "If Allman will not come to us, we must go to him. My son, you must go, but it will be dangerous."

"Where is the danger, Father?" asked the prince, "I can leave immediately with my royal guards and ride to Allman's village."

"But, my son," replied the king, "Allman will see you from across the valley. He will see you ride out from the castle in your royal robes and with your royal guards. He will fear that you are coming to arrest him and will run away to the Island of Caves beyond the Swamp Sea. There is only one way, and that is for you to travel alone. You must put aside your royal crown and robes and wear only the clothes of a simple servant. Travel quickly, my son," said the king. "The sun is low and soon darkness will fall and bring Darknor and his evil band of robbers onto the roads."

"Then I will leave at once, Father," said the prince.

Quickly, the prince exchanged his royal robes for a grubby servant's tunic and worn sandals. He wrapped a crystal apple into the folds of a leather pouch and placed it in a deep pocket inside his cloak. Then, pulling the hood over his head, he made his way to the hole in the wall and disappeared toward Allman's village.

On the other side of the valley Allman dashed along the road that leads toward his village. His mind raced. "I have to hide! I have to hide!" Then it came to him in a flash. "I'll hide in the Island of Caves beyond the Swamp Sea."

When he arrived at his cottage he rushed in. He slammed the door bolt across. Clang! Clunk!

His wife's jaw dropped. "Allman, Allman, what's wrong?"

"The king saw me trying to steal a crystal apple," he blurted out between gasping breaths.

"You tried to steal one of the king's crystal apples?" she gasped in horror. "But the penalty for that …"

"I'll be banished to the land of Dark Powers."

"Maybe the king doesn't know it was you."

Allman let out a great wail. "He knows! He called my name! It's just a matter of time before the guards hammer on our door."

He threw back the lid of a chest and began stuffing clothes into a travel bag.

"What are you doing?"

"I must leave now. I will hide on the Island of Caves."

"But it's so far away beyond the Swamp Sea."

"Yes, and far away from the king."

"But far away from me and everyone else too."

"You'll be alright. Stay with your father."

Allman's wife threw her arms out and grabbed him by the shoulders. She held him still. "But you can't leave now," she cried. "It's nearly evening and Darknor and his band of thugs will be out roaming the roads. They will steal whatever you have and take you as a slave. Stay until morning."

Allman looked at her and slowly nodded his head. "You are right. I'll wait and set out for the island at dawn."

The prince, meanwhile, had moved quickly along the road, but by now the sun had disappeared. As he neared Allman's village, darkness had already fallen across the valley. Gloom and shadows had swallowed up the countryside. Suddenly, the prince heard the clip, clop, clip, clop of approaching horses' hooves on the flinty road. He knew that this could be none other than the evil Darknor. He flung himself off the side of the road. But the roadside slope was steep and covered with ugly thorn bushes. The thorn bushes ripped and tore at his head and face as he tumbled downwards. He ended up in a muddy ditch at the bottom of the slope. He lay still, breathing as quietly as he could. He heard a foul voice cutting through the gloom.

"Who shall we visit tonight, my lord Darknor?"

An even more evil voice replied "Ah, let us pay a visit to this village ahead and see if there is anyone foolish enough to be out on my roadways at night."

The voices and the clip clop of the horses' hooves moved on toward Allman's village.

The prince was determined that nothing would stop him from completing the mission his father had given him. When all was quiet he began climbing back up the slope toward the road. But the stones on the slope were jagged and as sharp as nails. They cut at his hands and feet as he climbed upwards. Finally, the prince reached the road again. He brushed off some of the mud from his cloak and pushed on to the village. He made his way down the dark and empty streets. It was then, just as he turned into Mr Allman's street that out of the gloomy shadows sprang a pack of thugs. They surrounded the prince and there, suddenly leering at him, was the cruel, evil face of Darknor.

"Ahaa! Who have we here?" he hissed. "Who would be so foolish to travel my roads after dark?"

The prince, forgetting that he was not wearing his royal robes, stood tall. He raised his arm and pointed to Darknor. "Stand back, Darknor, you murderer and thief, for I am the son of the king."

"Haa!" snarled Darknor, "You! The son of the king! You are a mud-covered idiot knave. The king's son would never be so foolish as to venture from his castle in the darkness of the night without the protection of a legion of royal guards."

The prince fearlessly took a step toward Darknor, and once again commanded him. "Stand back, Darknor, for I am indeed the king's son." He raised his arm and hand still higher and in that instant, in the shadowy gloom, Darknor could see the flashing gleam of the royal ring upon the prince's finger.

He drew his breath, stepped back and snarled, "Hah! So you are indeed the king's son after all!" A wicked gleam lit up in his eyes and in a rasping snarl he hissed, "And you are the greater fool to venture into my darkness without a legion of your royal guards." He leaped forward and brought his club down across the head of the prince.

The prince slumped down onto the cold cobblestone road.

Darknor gloated over the unmoving form at his feet and then swung a heavy kick into the side of the motionless body. There was no movement. He began to shout and dance. "I have killed the son of the king! I have killed the heir. The kingdom is mine!" he shrieked. "Come quickly. There is much to be done. The kingdom is mine!" he screamed. Then he and his band of thugs disappeared into the murky shadows as quickly as they had come.

Now, if you and I were there, we would have thought that the body of the prince, lying still on the cold, cobblestone street was dead. But if you and I were there, we would have also been amazed to see that after a time, the prince stirred and slowly rose to his feet. He pulled his hood down over his bruised face and made his way down the street to Allman's cottage.

Allman heard a knock on the door and a quiet voice, "Allman, may I come in?"

Carefully and cautiously Allman unlocked the door and peered out into the darkness. Imagine his surprise when he saw a stooped and mud-covered figure standing quietly on his doorstep.

"Come in. Come in quickly!" Allman said in a hushed and hurried voice. "Don't you know you risk your life to be on the streets after darkness falls?" Allman pulled the visitor inside. He sat him at his table and brought out bread, cheese and drink.

The visitor noticed a bulging travel bag and a travelling staff in the corner.
"Are you planning a journey?" he asked.

Allman drew a deep breath and leaned forward.

He confessed how he longed to have a crystal apple more than anything else in the world. He told how he did not trust the king's offer to give him a crystal apple as a gift. "I don't trust the king or his son. It's all a trap to trick me into serving him," he mumbled. "I planned to get a crystal apple my way and not the king's way."

"But," he blurted out, "it all went wrong. The king saw me trying to steal a crystal apple. He even called out my name. His royal guards will surely come in the morning, hammer on my door, and drag me away to the land of Dark Powers." He paused and let out a long sad sigh. "I must flee to hide in the caverns on the Island of Caves. I'll set out as soon as the morning star has driven away darkness."

The visitor, who had listened carefully to Allman, suddenly rose to his feet. From a deep pocket on the inside of his cloak he pulled out a package. He handed it to Allman and said, "Please don't open this until I have gone." With that he moved to the door, stepped into the gloomy street and made his way safely back to the castle.

After he had left, Allman unwrapped the package. As the folds of the leather cloth fell back the crystal apple caught the single flickering candle flame and flashed a thousand dancing images around the walls and ceiling. Allman drew in his breath. He couldn't believe that here in his hands was the thing he most longed for in all the world, a priceless, shimmering, shining crystal apple. As he held it up to further admire its dazzling beauty a note fluttered to the floor. Allman picked it up and read it.

"Dear Mr Allman, because you would not come to me, I have come to you. Please accept my gift." It was signed with the signature of the king and sealed with the royal seal made from the king's own ring.

Allman was stunned.

Early the next morning, as the morning star drove away darkness, Allman began his journey, but he was not going to the Island of Caves. His determined steps took him instead across the valley toward the king's castle. He made his way through the majestic gates, down the splendid entrance hall and into the magnificent royal throne room. There the king and the prince sat side by side on their royal thrones.

Standing before the king, Allman stooped and began to bow his head. It was at that moment that his eye caught the eye of the prince. He was stunned with amazement as he realised that he was standing before the one who had visited him so unexpectedly the night before. His visitor had been none other than the prince! The bright morning light streaming into the royal throne room revealed what the mud splashed hood had hidden in Allman's dim candle lit room the night before. Allman could now see the deep thorn scars across the forehead and face of the prince. As he bent low to kneel he saw hands and feet that were scarred deep from the nail-sharp, flinty stones of the roadside. He realised that these were the feet that had risked the journey through the dangers of the night to come to him. These were the hands that had knocked on his door the night before and had given him a crystal apple to be his very own.

With head bowed low and tears streaming down his cheeks, Allman whispered between trembling sobs, "My king, I am so sorry. So sorry that I did not trust you." Then he went on in a choking whisper, "Will you please forgive me and let me serve you and your son forever?"

The king stood. The silence in the throne room grew deeper. Stooping down, the king placed his hand on Allman's shoulder. He raised him to his feet. Then he spoke in a voice both powerful and tender. "Allman," he said, "I forgive you. Forever you may serve us, and forever you will be our friend."

Then Allman did something quite unexpected. He reached into a deep pocket in his tunic. With an open and trembling hand he offered his crystal apple to the king. "My king," he said, "you must take this back. I don't deserve it. I never will."

"I know," said the king as he folded the outstretched fingers back around the crystal apple.

"Allman, this is my gift to you. Not because you deserve it but because I love you ... I always have."

The prince stepped forward and put his hand on Allman's shoulder.

"Come," he said. "Join us in the royal banquet hall."

You can get this and a variety of other great titles from Stone Table Books
www.stonetablebooks.com.
or Wipf and Stock Publishers
www.wipfandstock.com

Order online to get a copy shipped direct to you from a nearby supplier anywhere in the world.

Or you can contact the author
Email: barryandann@thelocks.net
Facebook: facebook.com/thecrystalapplestory

CPSIA information can be obtained
at www.ICGtesting.com
Printed in the USA
LVHW070943110922
728093LV00001B/15